RACCOONS IN THE CORN

A Children's Story by Jerilynn Henrikson
Illustration by Josh Finley

Farmer Baldridge loved his sweet corn. Every spring he planted a big patch between his house and the hedgerow. Farmer Baldridge was a nice man, small and quick with snappy brown eyes. A fringe of silver hair circled his shiny bald head. He was kind to his dog and loved his wife, but he was stingy with his corn. He carried buckets of tomatoes to the neighbors and shared cucumbers with his cousins, but he hoarded his golden corn like a miser.

Sometimes the raccoons in the hedgerow would take a few of the sweet, yummy ears. Farmer B. could always see when some ears were missing, and whenever he saw the hint of a pointy black nose or a bushy ringed tail, he shouted into the hedge, "Stay out of my corn, you thieving rascals."

Each February, he would sit in his granddaddy's old rocker by the fireplace and look through the seed catalogs to find his favorite varieties of sweet corn: Silver Queen, Peaches and Cream, Ambrosia, or Candy Corn. He checked the Farmer's Almanac, counted the days until spring, and waited until a day in late April or early May when the leaves on the hedge trees were as big as a squirrel's ear before planting his corn.

irst, he tilled the soil until it was soft and fine. Next, he set the tiller to make deep, even rows. Then he loaded his granddaddy's corn planter with Ambrosia seed corn and dropped the seeds into the rich, mounded earth. After three or four days, he began looking early each morning to see if the corn was coming up. He prayed for rain, hoed the weeds, and put a fresh red checked shirt on the scarecrow. At last, on the eighth day, he saw little green shoots. Every morning the shoots were several inches taller. They became stalks and, by summer, tassels had sprung from the tops where they danced in the Kansas wind and sprinkled pollen on the ears forming below.

Farmer B. was beginning to get excited about tasting those first sweet ears. He watched the silks on the ends of the ears because he knew that as soon as the silk dried into brown strings, the ears would be ready to harvest. He was proud that for five straight years his sweet corn had taken top prize at the county fair.

Farmer Baldridge was not the only one watching the corn. The family of raccoons who lived in the hedgerow watched too. In the dark of night, Papa Raccoon would waddle into the corn patch and sniff the corn. His sensitive black nose would tell him when the corn was perfectly ripe. Then the family planned to have a feast.

One early morning, Farmer B. told his wife, "This year those pesky raccoons

are not getting any of my corn." She just smiled at him and shook her springy gray curls. He went to Bluestem Farm and Ranch Supply and bought electric fencing and put it around the corn patch. He tied shiny tin can lids to the fence to dance and blink in the wind and scare the raccoons away. He strung a long extension cord from the house and hooked up a radio tuned to the opera station to fool the critters into thinking someone large and lusty was singing in the corn. He even installed motion lights at each corner of the patch.

Farmer Baldridge bragged to his wife, "Those raccoons will not be stealing any more of my corn. The lights will scare them, the music will startle them, the can lids will confuse them, and the electric fence will shock the masks right off their sneaky little faces." He slapped his thigh with glee.

"Tell you what, Mrs. B. Let's load up the fishing poles, hitch up the camper, get in the pick-up, and drive to the lake for the weekend. By Monday, the kernels will be full and plump, and until then, my corn is safe."

"Good idea dear," she replied, "a break from corn. And while you are fishing, I can finish designing the quilt I'm planning for the county fair. In your honor, I'm calling the pattern 'Farmer B's Corn Patch.'"

he raccoons who lived in the hedgerow were curious about all the changes in the corn patch. At dark that night, Papa Raccoon rolled toward the patch in his usual rocking way. As soon as he cleared the hedge row, the motion lights glared from each corner.

Papa Raccoon whirred a raccoon warning and flattened to the ground. He lay still, and the lights went out. When he raised his head, the lights came on again. Down he went, out went the lights. Up he came, on came the lights. Up, down, on, off, up, down, on, off. But nothing else happened. So Papa Raccoon rolled on toward the electric fence.

"This wire has a strange, hot smell," he informed the rest of the family. Then he leaned on some tall pig weeds until they dropped onto the fence and flattened the wire to the ground. As soon as the weeds fell, the motion lights glared from each corner. But, inspired by Papa Raccoon's confidence, the raccoon family trooped across the pig weed bridge into the corn patch. Papa Raccoon sniffed several ears and announced, "The corn is ready!"

Junior Raccoon found the radio and pushed the buttons with his quick, clever hands until he tuned in a country western station. He loved Willie Nelson. Mama Raccoon ooohed and aaahed over the pretty can lids. "Look," she said, "party decorations. Let's have a corn party!"

She began organizing immediately. She assigned the twins, Milly and Lilly, to gather up some acorn cups and make sumac tea. She told Cousin Ringo and Uncle Zorro to help Papa knock down the stalks and put Little Red and Big Tom in charge of husking. Soon the party was hopping, and raccoons from all over Route Five were hurrying to Farmer Baldridge's corn patch. The motion lights flashed a disco beat as the raccoons danced the Texas Two Step, the Virginia Reel, and the Kansas Cornhusking Hustle. They munched until dawn and ate every kernel.

On Monday morning, Farmer Baldridge opened the door of the camper, checked the weather, and woke his wife even earlier than usual. "Today is the day," he announced, "time to get home and put up the corn. I checked before we left and by my well tuned internal corn-o-meter, today the ears should be perfect for the freezer: plump, tender, and sweet as sugar. We'll be enjoying corn all winter," he said, licking his lips: "Creamed corn for Thanksgiving, corn casserole at Christmas, and corn muffins every Sunday morning."

"Congratulations, sighed his wife. You made it two and a half days without mentioning, seeing, or touching CORN." As soon as they pulled in the barnyard, Farmer B. went to the shed to get his baskets and headed for the corn patch. What he saw made him drop his jaw and his baskets. No corn stocks stood, no ears were untouched, every kernel was gone.

He clenched his fists, his teeth, even his eyelashes. He began to shake. He jumped up and down. He threw his straw hat to the ground and stomped it flat. He gave a shout that shook the hedge trees and echoed along the creek...

His wife heard the ruckus and came running. "Oh my," was all she said when she saw the ruined corn patch.

"Is that all you can say?" shouted Farmer Baldridge.

Mrs. B. gave her husband a long, hard stare, and then she looked down at her shoes a long moment before lifting her curls. When she looked up, she was grinning, "Well, frozen nibblets from the market are pretty good, and next year, you can plant two patches: one for us, and one for the raccoons. It's about time you learned to share."

Farmer Baldridge glared at her as she smiled. Then he began to smile too. Soon he grinned his lop-sided grin. Then he began to chuckle and then laugh. Next, he gave his wife a big hug, and said, "I'll do just that."

Mrs. B. squeezed his hand. "Maybe next year they'll invite us. It must have been quite a party! And look, dear, at the crazy pattern of the fallen stalks and the soft yellow of the scattered husks. I am changing my quilt pattern to 'Raccoons in the Corn' and I'll bet your corn will still take first prize at the fair."

CORN RECIPES

Sunday Sweet Corn Muffins

1 cup cornmeal
1 cup all-purpose flour
2 teaspoons baking powder
1 teaspoon baking soda
1/2 teaspoon salt
½ cup sugar
1 egg, beaten
1/3 cup honey
1/4 cup melted butter
1 cup milk
1 cup thawed frozen sweet corn

Preheat oven to 400 degrees F. Grease muffin pan or line with paper muffin liners.

In a large bowl, mix corn meal, flour, baking powder, soda, salt and sugar. Add egg, honey, butter, milk and corn; stir gently to combine.

Spoon batter into prepared muffin cups.

Bake at 400 degrees for 15 to 20 minutes, or until a toothpick inserted into a muffin comes out clean.

Farmer B's Favorite Creamed Corn

½ gal. package frozen
   sweet corn thawed
1 stick butter
8 oz. package cream cheese
garlic salt to taste (1/2-1 tsp

Mix together in large sauce pan over low/med. Heat
Stir frequently until hot
Simmer on lowest heat for five minutes

Christmas Corn Casserole

2 eggs, beaten
1 quart bag frozen sweet corn thawed
1 cup sour cream
1/4 cup butter, melted
1 1/2 cups shredded Cheddar cheese
1/2 cup chopped onion
1 (4 ounce) can diced green chilies
1 small jar chopped pimento peppers
1 (8.5 ounce) package dry corn muffin mix

Preheat oven to 350 degrees Grease a 2 quart casserole dish.
Combine eggs, corn, cream cheese and melted butter. Stir in, cheese, onion, pimento, and chilies. Stir in the corn muffin mix until just moistened.
Bake in a preheated 350 degree oven for 75 minutes; or until an inserted knife comes out clean and the top is golden.

Made in the USA
Charleston, SC
22 April 2011